SECRET SPY SOCIETY

the CASE of the MISSING CHEETAH

Veronica Mang

VIKING

VIKING
An imprint of Penguin Random House LLC, New York

First published in the United States of America by Viking,
an imprint of Penguin Random House LLC, 2021

Visit us online at penguinrandomhouse.com.

LIBRARY OF CONGRESS CATALOGING-IN-PUBLICATION DATA IS AVAILABLE.

Printed in the United States of America

ISBN 9780593204351

10 9 8 7 6 5 4 3 2 1

Design by Kate Renner
Text set in New Baskerville ITC Infant

For Mom and Dad,
who taught me to dream and to laugh

To,
Annu

Hope you enjoy
the Book !!

from:
Adarsh Anna...

Chapter ONE

All throughout history, there have been lady spies who have single-handedly changed the world. They are famed for their wit, admired for their charm, and, of course, applauded for their natural skills in espionage. Each lady spy had her own special skill. Some were trained to be expert codebreakers. Some could interpret body language or signals that were meant to be secret. Some were masters of martial arts and could jump, dash, leap, and loop their way to safety. And some were masters of deception and could

charm their way out of dangerous situations or into mysterious ones.

This story is about them . . . but it is not only about them. It is also about three little girls named Peggy, Rita, and Dot. They, too, had their own special skills, and on a very rainy night in a very rainy town, they found themselves in a very peculiar situation.

In the little girls' "clubhouse," things were a bit too quiet. The spy club met routinely in Rita's attic, but what was the point anymore? The clubhouse phone hadn't rung for weeks, and it was collecting dust.

Usually, the girls' skills were put to use solving mysteries, like stolen ballet slippers or cryptic notes left in sidewalk chalk. Tonight, however, the girls were just bored. All that was left to do was to sit around the clubhouse and play some sort of game to pass the time.

On this evening, that was Go Fish, and Rita was taking a very long time on her next move.

Rita, who was one for planning, calculating, and figuring out, was trying very hard to decide whom to request an ace from.

Peggy, who was one for charm, chatting, and spunkiness, was practicing card tricks. Card tricks can be useful in sticky situations

RITA

PEGGY

or for pranks or for occupying yourself when your friend is taking too long.

Dot, who was one for acrobatics, crafts, and doing things with her hands, chose to occupy herself by building a giant card tower. It got taller and taller and taller and taller . . .

DOT

"Ah-ha!" said Rita. Finally, a decision had been made.

WHOOSH!

went the card tower.

"My tower!" cried Dot. The stacks
of cards crumbled and tumbled, and
the wind swept them up into the air
and right out of the open window.

The girls rushed after them and watched as the cards floated away into the storm outside.

"Well," sighed Peggy, "there goes our fun." They were just about to turn away when something odd happened. Through the fog and the rain, they saw a woman under a yellow umbrella walking unusually fast down the street. They supposed that this was not out of the ordinary. But in the middle of the night? And in the middle of a storm?

"How odd," said Rita.

"How peculiar," said Dot.

"And how absolutely unignorable," said Peggy.

There was nothing to discuss—the girls swept into action. They had, after all, just lost their only entertainment, and perhaps it was time to find their own mystery.

At this point in their sleuthing pursuits, the girls had gone on so many adventures that they had an unspoken routine. For example, Dot was usually the stunt girl, because she moved very fast and swift, more so than most children her age. She sped around the room and collected all the necessary materials: a flashlight, Rita's notebook, Peggy's sunglasses, their rain shoes, a snack—all the essentials. Dot was usually done before the other girls and would stand impatient and fidgety until they were ready.

A magnifying glass, for up-close inspections

A screwdriver for sticky situations

A private composition book, for super-secret notes

PRIVATE! PEGGY RITA DOT

Rita was the problem solver. She made sure all the details were figured out. Where were they going? Did they need to bring any books? Know any codes? Plot any maps? She always had a stockpile of information handy that made her excellent at figuring out tough problems. All of these brainy and mathematical things came very easily for Rita.

Peggy was the performer.

A yo-yo, for looking inconspicuous

A harmonica, for when spies have the blues

Binoculars, for peeking secretly

Pens and pencils, for note-taking

Scissors and string, for quick inventions

She could talk her way into or out of any situation, and convince even the most cranky, skeptical adults. She always made sure that they had an explanation to get out of any sticky situation and were fully equipped with disguises. Hats, hoods, hairdos—she would pack sunglasses and extra outfits to hide in plain sight. Only in case of emergency, of course, but every good spy needs to prepare. Today, their needs were few but specific: raincoats and headgear for both cover and function, since it was storming.

A flashlight, for rainy nights like tonight

A sandwich, for snack emergencies

Outside, the rain poured down on them with loud PLUNK, PLUNKS on their hoods and hats and helmets. They trailed behind the umbrellaed figure, following through twisty, turny streets.

The umbrellaed lady was taking an odd route, but they tried their best to keep up.

Their feet splish-splash-splish-splashed in puddles as they shuffled down the street. Peggy's foot landed on the wet sidewalk, but instead of the normal splash or plop, her foot landed with a

CLINK!

"Wait up!" she whisper-yelled to the other girls. They looped back around, and Dot pointed the flashlight down at Peggy's boots. They crowded over as she reached down and pulled a long muddy something out of the puddle.

"A stick?" asked Rita.

"A fork?" asked Dot.

"Even better," said Peggy, wiping off the mud. "A very fancy and very important-looking clue!"

They gathered around and stared at the shiny gold thing in Peggy's hand. A fountain pen! And etched into it, they saw two elegant letters: *N.K.*

"N.K.?" the girls wondered aloud.

Somehow, this felt familiar. N.K. . . . N.K. . . . The girls didn't think they knew anyone with the initials N.K., did they?

"Oh no!" Rita gasped. "Where did the woman go?"

"I think we might have lost her," Dot said. They all stopped. They had a hard time seeing anything through the storm. Dot pulled out her binoculars and peered down the street, but there was no sign of the yellow umbrella.

18

"I have an idea!" she said. Before they could say anything, she hopped like a cat onto the fence, then the garage, then the trellis, and then the roof. Leap, jump, climb—all of a sudden Dot was on the tippy-top of the nearest house!

She pointed and called down, "I see her!"

Rita pulled out her compass. "That's northeast!"

In a moment, Dot was back on the ground and they were off speeding down the street.

They continued onward through the storm, following the yellow umbrella.

Past puddles and sidewalk cracks.

Past quiet houses where people slept.

They followed so far that they didn't even recognize

the tall houses lining the crooked cobblestone streets.

After a few blocks, the umbrellaed woman stopped next to a very normal-looking door on a very normal-looking street. The girls crouched behind a bush and waited, eyes and ears extra-focused. The woman, still under the umbrella, leaned in and rang the doorbell.

Once . . . twice . . . three times . . . again . . . and again . . . and again . . .

"That's strange," Peggy said. The girls could barely hear the ringing over the steady patter of rain, but they listened very closely. Why was she ringing the doorbell over and over?

Rita listened intently. Something felt . . . familiar. "I know this," she said. "This isn't normal doorbell ringing. This is a code!"

She dug into her bag and pulled out a notebook. She flipped until she opened to a page that was carefully labeled "Morse Code."

There were short rings and long rings, which translated into certain letters of the alphabet when they were combined.

Long, short. Short. Short, long, long.

"N-E-W. . . . I-N-T-E-L. . . . N-K." Rita spelled out, translating with her eyes on her notes.

"N.K.? Again?" asked Dot.

"I wonder what that means," Peggy said.

Rita was puzzled. "I'm not sure. But she looks like someone who is up to something."

The girls snuck in closer when, suddenly, the flashlight dropped out of Dot's hand and landed with a horrible THWACK!

"AHHH!"

cried the woman as she dropped her umbrella.

"AHHH!"

cried the girls.

Everyone stood looking at one another. The mysterious woman stared at them with wide eyes, turned away, and dove for her umbrella.

"Nope!" Dot swooped in and snatched it away.

The girls circled closer and wiped the rain out of their eyes. Peggy held up the pen.

"Miss Khan?!"

For there, standing in front of them, was none other than their very own teacher.

Chapter TWO

"**W**hat?" Peggy exclaimed.

"How?" Dot shrieked.

". . . and why?" Rita chirped.

Miss Khan was frozen. It was very strange for the girls to spot their teacher outside of school, but judging by the look on Miss Khan's face, it was even stranger for her to spot them. "I'm happy to see you! But you sure gave me quite a scare. What on earth are you doing way out here in the middle of the night?"

Dot and Rita glanced side-eyed at Peggy. "We . . . well . . . we, uh . . . we needed to . . . get a new deck of cards! Yes, you see, we lost ours earlier today. It was tragic! A freaky wind in Rita's attic blew them—whoosh! Right out the window!" Peggy's eyes were big and full of theatrics. Rita, Dot, and even Miss Khan were completely absorbed by her story. "And you know how antsy we get when we have nothing to do, right? So, of course, we absolutely needed to get that new deck of cards right away. And you know how this town is— everything closes so early! The only place open this late is that store, you know, that one way over there on the other side of town. Sad, really. So few options around here!"

Peggy took a deep breath.

"Anyhow, we're walking along and we find this beautiful pen in a puddle, and then we see you! Up ahead. Of course we didn't know it was you, but we figured, 'Oh boy, this beautiful pen might belong to that lady up there, we'd better catch her!' So, you know, we caught up, and, uh. . . . Here's your pen!" Peggy gave a sheepish grin and thrust the pen forward. "N.K. That's you!"

Miss Khan blinked. "Please, my dears, do come inside."

They went through the doors of the mysterious house. Miss Khan warmed a kettle on the stove. Rita was wandering around the room and, of course, paused at the bookshelf. There were all sorts of fascinating books: books about architecture and astronomy and Antarctica and aerospace engineering. There was even a book about books! She pulled out a particularly fat and interesting one called *Cryptography, Ciphers, and the Art of Codes* and plopped it on the table.

Dot, meanwhile, sped around the room, picking up trinkets and putting them down and then whizzing to the next shelf. She made her way from thing to thing until she came to a door that was almost hidden in the corner. It was open a crack, and she peeked through. There was a room full of other women in fancy dresses. Twinklings of piano and trumpets drifted from inside. Some of the women were singing and a few were gathered around a table. Dot thought they looked very serious, like there was something important going on.

"Who are they?" asked Dot.

Miss Khan hurried over.

"That's my . . . dance troupe. We get together every now and then to practice our routines." She quickly shut the door.

In a few minutes, Miss Khan had produced three steaming cups of hot chocolate. The girls, naturally, added marshmallows.

Peggy slinked into her chair. "So, Miss Khan, I never got to ask. What exactly were you doing . . ."

Rita shoved her with a pointy elbow and gave her a look that said *please stop talking or you're going to get us caught!*

". . . with . . . with all this hot chocolate? I would've pegged you as a tea person." An expert mid-sentence switch.

Miss Khan blinked.

"I . . . I am a huge fan of choco-late. A fanatic. Milk chocolate. Dark chocolate. Even white chocolate. I'll take chocolate over boring tea anytime. Wouldn't you?"

The girls nodded in perfect synchronization.

Miss Khan looked satisfied, but the girls knew there was still more to the story. Rita looked at Miss Khan, then at the fat book that was on the table, and then once more around the room. There were too many coincidences. Like Peggy, all she wanted to do was ask Miss Khan a thousand questions until she could say for certain what was going on. But their whole mission would be ruined if they got busted now! So, instead of asking more questions, she sipped and chatted until it was time to go home.

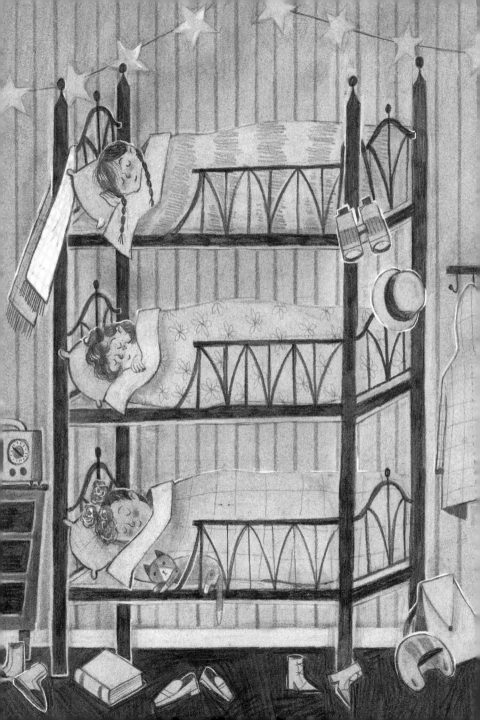

That night, the girls slept at Rita's with their bellies full of sugar. But somewhere, floating in their imaginations between the twinkling of piano and the warmth of the cocoa, was the question: What was behind that door in the kitchen?

—＊—＊—＊—

The next day, the girls lazed around the clubhouse, still thinking about their mysterious encounter with Miss Khan. Peggy was on the floor, paging through the *Daily Herald*. Most girls their age didn't read the *Daily Herald*, but they were a spy club, and it was of the utmost importance for them to stay informed.

Today, however, they were feeling sluggish after their late night, and because of this, Peggy was looking for the comics section.

"What could it all mean?" Rita wondered out loud, for what felt like the hundredth time that afternoon.

Peggy let out a long whine. "Would you please let it go?" How exasperating!

Dot was practicing handstands in the corner. "Yeah, Rita, it was no big deal. That cocoa was the most exciting part, and besides"—she cartwheeled out of her handstand and then launched into another one—"it's Miss Khan. She's just our teacher. That's all there is to it."

"Yeah!" Peggy snorted. "It's not like she has some sort of other life."

Dot chuckled and joined in. "Ha! Yeah, or Miss Khan is secretly an alien!"

Rita glared at them. This time her look said, *You're not funny and you stink.*

"Or she has a room of pirate treasure!"

"Or she is a mad scientist!"

"Or a world-famous movie star!"

Dot tumbled from her acrobatics in a fit of giggles. "Or, I've got it—she has a secret identity and we accidentally caught her!"

"Ha, secret identity." Peggy snickered and flipped to the next page. Then her giggles stopped. "What in the world!" she cried.

Rita and Dot rushed over to see what the excitement was. They both gasped when they saw a familiar face right there on page six.

"That's one of the women from behind the door!" Rita gasped. "I knew it!"

In the newspaper was a photograph of a beautiful woman in a feathery cap. Underneath was her name, Josephine Baker, spelled out in thick black letters. The headline read, "Beloved performer, socialite, and philanthropist suspected of ties to espionage."

"Espionage?!" The girls were stunned and intrigued. Without a moment's hesitation, Dot grabbed the flashlight and

Rita grabbed the radio. Peggy didn't know what to grab, but she hopped up anyway because this was all very exciting and she wanted to be helpful. Their new mission was clear.

In a hurry, they laced their galoshes, buttoned their raincoats, and sped out of the house with the torn newspaper page in their hands.

They traced their steps back past sidewalk cracks and puddles, sleeping people and crooked streets, until they found the yellow house on the gray block. The three little girls raced up the steps. Peggy, always the honorary spokesperson, stepped forward and summoned three great

KNOCK

KNOCK

KNOCKS.

The door opened a crack. Out peered two blinking eyes.

"Miss Khan?"

The door opened some more.

"Girls! What brings you back here today?"

Peggy took a deep breath.

"We know that you're spies."

Miss Khan blinked at them.

"Please, my dears, do come inside."

The house was full of wonders. All around them, the women whom they had spotted last night were doing lots of interesting things, like listening to radios and pointing to maps. Some were playing pool or piano or having lively conversations. It was a Secret Spy Society.

Mary Jane Richards Denman: formerly enslaved, and a very courageous undercover expert

Virginia Hall: frequently undercover and in disguise

Yolande Beekman: very kind, wireless code expert

FLIGHT

ART

Cecily Lefort, code name *Alice*: skilled at code-breaking, sailing, and high-society manners

Violette Szabo, code name *Louise*: expert navigator, escape artist, and joke-teller

50

Nancy Wake: self-taught journalist, charm master, and *fiercely* skilled martial artist

Odette Hallowes, code name *Lise*: seemingly ordinary but a trained combat fighter

Sarah Aaronsohn: heroic leader, even among already-heroic spies

Sarah Emma Edmonds, code name *Franklin*: went undercover as a man for several years

Christine Granville: renowned socialite and master of charm

Barreling from room to room, they almost smashed headfirst into a tall, slender woman.

"Who are these three?" she asked. The woman peered down at them through long eyelashes. A smile danced across her face. It was Josephine, the woman from the newspaper!

"I'm Rita!"

"I'm Dot!"

"I'm Peggy! And we want to be spies, too!"

Miss Khan followed in behind them.

"It's true," she said. "Their skills are quite promising and they followed me all the way here yesterday, even in the middle of the storm!"

Josephine gazed down at them, thinking. Her nose wrinkled.

"Spies, you say? Well, well . . . we may just have a job for you after all."

Chapter THREE

Josephine walked over to a tall bookshelf, her dress glittering as she walked. She reached up to the highest shelf, which was packed full of overstuffed files, and pulled out a folder from the "J" section.

"You see, some weeks ago, my precious Chiquita the cheetah was stolen right out from under our noses. One moment she was there and the next—poof!

Gone just like that. And we think we may have a lead on who did it."

She pulled out a file full of typed notes, scraps of paper with jaggedy handwriting, and lots of shaky photographs taken at odd angles.

"We've been watching our strange neighbor Mr. Jenkins for a while. We know for sure that he is up to some sort of crooked business in his crooked house. Your job, little spies, is to scout out any signs of our precious Chiquita. Unfortunately, Mr. Jenkins is quite aware of us. But not you! You are just what we need."

The girls puffed their chests. "Count us in!"

Peggy, Rita, and Dot got to work. Rita grabbed her notebook and started scribbling some notes. "What will Mr. Jenkins think when he sees us?"

Peggy closed her eyes and thought hard with the silly part of her brain that was good for inventing tricks or pranks.

She opened her eyes. "Little girls. Innocent and

ordinary little girls. What if we use that to our advantage?"

"What do you mean?" asked Dot.

The solution, they decided, was cookies. Scout cookies, to be exact. Before they embarked on their adventure, Josephine and Miss Khan gathered them together.

"Please be careful," said Miss Khan. "And take this." She handed them a small radio. "It's a walkie-talkie in case you need help."

Josephine leaned down. "Remember to only observe Mr. Jenkins. A good spy does not meddle; she only watches."

They loaded up their wagon with boxes and boxes of Peanut Butter Patties and wheeled it down the dark street to the door of an even darker house. Peggy reached up with one shaking finger and pressed the doorbell.

The door opened with a creak. The girls could hardly make out the figure standing in the shadows. He leaned over them, eyes hidden behind black glasses.

"Hello," he rasped.

Another deep breath from Peggy.

"Hello, sir, how are you? Can I offer you some Scout cookies? They raise money for our annual camping trip, which is a total blast! Would you care to buy any today?" Her words tumbled out quickly, but only Rita and Dot could tell that she was nervous.

He peered down over his mustache.

"I'm not interested." He began to close the door.

"But they are Peanut Butter Patties," Peggy insisted. "Our most delicious cookie."

He paused. "Did you say Peanut Butter Patties? Well . . . give me just a moment." He disappeared back into the house.

"Now's our chance!" whispered Peggy, poking the other two. They took a deep breath and plunged into the darkness.

Inside the doorway, Dot flicked on the flashlight. With each step, the floorboards let out a squeak that was far too loud for such a secretive mission.

The hallways of the house bent at odd angles, with strange staircases and unusual passageways. The girls tried to keep track of their path, but even Rita feared that they were lost.

Finally, they emerged into a long corridor. Dot led the way. "Chiquita! Chiquita!" she called softly into the dark. Down the hallway she stepped on the thick rug, trying her best to stop the floor from squeaking. At the end of the hallway was a door, half-opened.

She approached, grimacing
as it made a soft

They stepped through.

They ran over to the cage. "Poor Chiquita!" Peggy whispered. "This is scary! Look at all these terrible things on the wall. What is he going to do to her?"

"No time to worry about that," said Dot. She pulled a screwdriver out of her pocket and began to poke and prod at the lock.

Meanwhile, Rita pulled out the walkie-talkie from Josephine. "Lady Spies!" she called through the static. "We need help! This is more serious than we thought!"

The girls huddled around the cage. Rita handed Dot tools while Peggy comforted Chiquita, who was pacing around the cage looking very, very panicked. Time felt too slow and too fast all at once, and their hearts were beating very quickly. After what felt like hours and hours, the lock finally popped open with a

CLICK!

"Good job, Dot!" Rita and Peggy sighed with relief. Dot was about to open the cage when they heard footsteps approaching.

They whipped around and, to their horror, Mr. Jenkins appeared in the doorway.

"Well, well, well . . . how on earth did you little ones end up in here?"

The girls jumped up in front of the cage. For the first time, even Peggy was at a loss for words.

"We . . . we . . . we needed to use the bathroom, and we got lost," Peggy stuttered.

Mr. Jenkins tsked. "Now, now," he said. "Let's not be foolish."

He took a few steps forward. Chiquita growled.

Behind Mr. Jenkins, the girls noticed
movement. Flashes of coats and feathers
and buttons danced through the shadows.
The Lady Spies!

Mr. Jenkins took another few steps. "You see, little ones, I'm starting to think you might not really be Scouts. Now, what am I to do about that?"

Rita's mind was racing. There must be a solution. She thought of the cage door. And then she thought of the book she had seen back at the Secret Spy Society. Codes!

Rita grabbed the flashlight from Dot's hand and began clicking furiously. On, off. On, off. Short flashes, long, long flashes. "L-O-C-K . . . I-S . . . O-P-E-N . . ."

Mr. Jenkins chuckled. "Poor little girl! So nervous that you can't even turn on your flashlight!"

Behind Mr. Jenkins, the girls could just make out Miss Khan. When she saw Rita's message, her eyes widened. Rita knew she understood!

The Lady Spies crept forward from the shadows, moving so quietly and expertly that they didn't make a peep. Mr. Jenkins took a few more steps forward, mustache twitching. And then, all of a sudden . . .

CRASH! BANG! BOOM!

The Lady Spies burst from the shadows.

POP! POW! CLANG!

And just like that, Chiquita was out of the cage and Mr. Jenkins was in it!

The Lady Spies gathered around the girls. They gave big warm hugs. "Thank goodness you're okay!" Miss Khan said.

Peggy pulled away. "We're just happy that we made it in time to help Chiquita!"

Off to the side, Josephine and her precious pet cheetah were reunited. It's a little-known fact that cheetahs can purr, and on this occasion everyone could hear a loud grumble bubbling from Chiquita's chest as Josephine squeezed her into a tight hug.

Mr. Jenkins rattled the cage. "You can't do this!" he howled.

Chiquita let out a

GROOOWL!

and snapped with her pointy teeth.

Josephine waltzed over. "Yes, dear Jenkins, we can!" She gave Chiquita a pat on the head. "Let's get out of here." The spies and the girls retraced their steps out through the crooked house.

Back at the Secret Spy Society, Miss Khan once again heated a kettle and the girls once again sat around the table. But this time, all of the Lady Spies joined them.

"Girls, you did excellent work," said Josephine.

"Very clever," added Miss Granville.

"Quick on your feet!" chimed Mrs. Lefort.

"So brave!" said Ms. Aaronsohn.

"Fabulous and stupendous!" declared Miss Khan. "As well done as any Lady Spy!" She brought the hot chocolate out on a tray. "Truly, we could not have done this without you!"

The ladies sipped. The girls slurped. Chiquita munched. They knew she would like marshmallows, and there was an unmistakable grin on her furry face.

When the hot chocolates were finished, Josephine cleared her throat with a smile.

"You know," she began, "we were thinking. There are some missions that are more perfectly suited for little girls."

Peggy, Rita, and Dot sat up a little straighter.

"Your skills could be quite useful to us. We have many mysteries left to solve. Maybe it's time we started a new branch of our Secret Spy Society. What do you think of the Petite Private Eyes?"

And that's how the Petite Private Eyes began. Rita, Peggy, and Dot wouldn't live happily ever after, but why would they want to? The girls had clues to find, people to meet, and mysteries to solve. As a matter of fact . . .

RING! RING!

AUTHOR'S NOTE

Although the setting of Secret Spy Society is fictional, the characters are not. There have been countless female spies throughout history. Many of them pushed the boundaries of what was considered acceptable for women. They were good at lots of other things, too. Some of them were dancers who could twirl their way through tricky situations. Some were skilled at martial arts or parachuting or flying planes. Others were amazing musicians or teachers or masters of disguise. In this story, I focused on two famous lady spies: Noor Khan and Josephine Baker.

NOOR INAYAT KHAN, of Indian and American descent, was a quiet British author of stories and poems for small children—which is why I imagined she might have been a wonderful teacher for Rita, Peggy, and Dot. She could play lots of instruments, including the harp! She was a pacifist, which means she didn't believe in fighting, but when she saw the violence

and suffering during World War II, she knew she needed to help. While she was being trained for the military, many of her male officers didn't think she was up for the job, but she proved them wrong and was recruited as a wireless operator, connecting London with the rest of Europe through coded languages. Eventually, she was the last remaining soldier at her post, but she refused to give in or reveal any secrets, even after she was kidnapped and sent to a concentration camp. She remained brave and her final word was rumored to be "liberty."

JOSEPHINE BAKER

was an African American dancer, performer, and master of charm. She used her abilities to mingle with socialites and officials to obtain the most classified secrets and aid the French Resistance during World War II. She was able to travel the world as an entertainer, but no one ever knew she was a spy. Josephine did lots of things that women weren't supposed to do during her time—she adopted lots of children, refused to perform in places that prohibited African Americans, and loved whomever she wanted to. She was famous for her fabulous costumes, and she really did have a pet cheetah named Chiquita!

Even though the real Lady Spies lived at different points in history, I dreamed of one magical place where they could exist all at once, solving mysteries and sharing laughs together. I hope that their bravery and kindness can inspire a new generation of readers who find themselves holding this very book.

ABOUT THE OTHER LADY SPIES

SARAH AARONSOHN (1890-1917)

Syria. Founded and led an underground network of Jewish spies during World War I.

YOLANDE BEEKMAN (1911-1944)

Great Britain. Spoke several languages, which made her especially useful for secretive communications for the Special Operations Executive during World War II.

MARY JANE RICHARDS DENMAN (C. 1840-UNKNOWN)

United States. Also known as Mary Bowser, Denman was a freed slave who went undercover in the Confederate South to fight against slavery as a Union Army spy.

SARAH EMMA EDMONDS (1841-1898)

Canada. Disguised herself as a man to help fight against slavery in the Civil War and work as a spy for the Union Army.

CHRISTINE GRANVILLE (1908-1952)

Poland. Also known as Krystyna Skarbek, she was known for her glamour, her style, and her ability to charm everyone (even guard dogs) as she worked for the Special Operations Executive during World War II.

VIRGINIA HALL (1906-1982)

United States. Worked for the American Office of Strategic Services and the CIA after World War II, along with other organizations. She lost one of her legs in a hunting accident, but her prosthetic leg (named Cuthbert) made her excellent at undercover missions.

ODETTE HALLOWES (1912-1995)

Great Britain. Proved herself invaluable to her team at the Special Operations Executive despite her nervous demeanor. Also a mother of three girls, she survived the Ravensbrück concentration camp.

CECILY LEFORT (1900-1945)

Great Britain. Served in the Women's Auxiliary Air Force and for the Special Operations Executive during World War II. She had excellent manners and liked sailing boats and riding horses.

VIOLETTE SZABO (1921–1945)

France. Worked for the Special Operations Executive during World War II and was highly trained in many specialties like navigation, demolition, and parachuting. (She could also tell very good jokes.)

NANCY WAKE (1912–2011)

New Zealand. Celebrated for her skills in combat and infamous for her sassy wit, she joined the French Resistance and the Special Operations Executive in World War II.

Morse code is a simple language that is formed with only dots and dashes. When combined together in a specific order, these dots and dashes signify letters, which can be used to form words and secret messages. Before there were telephones, Morse code was used to send messages over long distances using radio and telegraph devices, and the language is still used today by sailors and pilots.

Messages in Morse code can be written on paper or signaled with other things like blinking lights and short precise sounds. For example, when Rita sends a message with a flashlight, a dot is a quick flash of light and a dash is a longer flash. Or when Miss Khan sends a message with a doorbell, a dot is a short, quick *ding*, and a dash is a longer, drawn-out sound. Morse code is perfect for sharing top-secret information with close friends, confidantes, and fellow spies.

• = quick   — = slow

A = • —
B = — • • •
C = — • — •
D = — • •
E = •
F = • • — •
G = — — •
H = • • • •
I = • •

J = • — — —
K = — • —
L = • — • •
M = — —
N = — •
O = — — —
P = • — — •
Q = — — • —

R = • — •
S = —
T = • —
U = • • —
V = • • • —
W = • — —
X = — • • —
Y = — • — —
Z = — — • •